MAR - - 2022

Farah Rocks

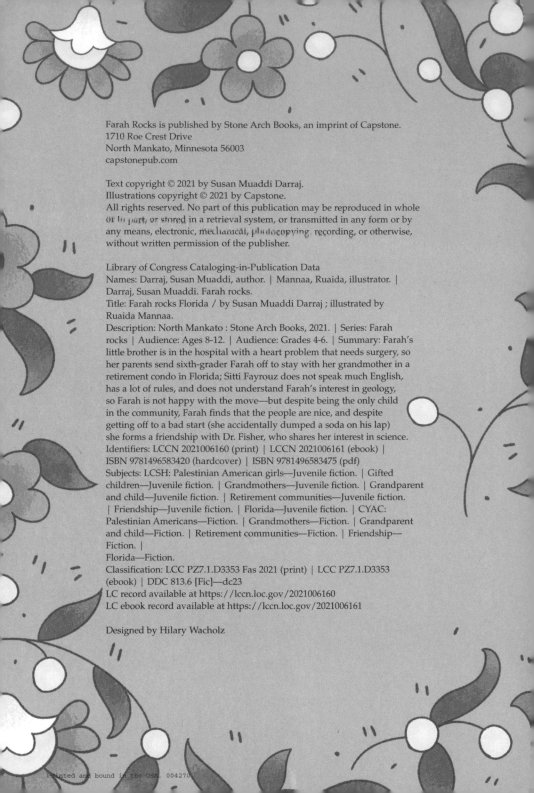

Farah Rocks is published by Stone Arch Books, an imprint of Capstone.
1710 Roe Crest Drive
North Mankato, Minnesota 56003
capstonepub.com

Library of Congress Cataloging-in-Publication Data
Names: Darraj, Susan Muaddi, author. | Mannaa, Ruaida, illustrator. |
Darraj, Susan Muaddi. Farah rocks.
Title: Farah rocks Florida / by Susan Muaddi Darraj ; illustrated by
Ruaida Mannaa.
Description: North Mankato : Stone Arch Books, 2021. | Series: Farah
rocks | Audience: Ages 8-12. | Audience: Grades 4-6. | Summary: Farah's
little brother is in the hospital with a heart problem that needs surgery, so
her parents send sixth-grader Farah off to stay with her grandmother in a
retirement condo in Florida; Sitti Fayrouz does not speak much English,
has a lot of rules, and does not understand Farah's interest in geology,
so Farah is not happy with the move—but despite being the only child
in the community, Farah finds that the people are nice, and despite
getting off to a bad start (she accidentally dumped a soda on his lap)
she forms a friendship with Dr. Fisher, who shares her interest in science.
Identifiers: LCCN 2021006160 (print) | LCCN 2021006161 (ebook) |
ISBN 9781496583420 (hardcover) | ISBN 9781496583475 (pdf)
Subjects: LCSH: Palestinian American girls—Juvenile fiction. | Gifted
children—Juvenile fiction. | Grandmothers—Juvenile fiction. | Grandparent
and child—Juvenile fiction. | Retirement communities—Juvenile fiction.
| Friendship—Juvenile fiction. | Florida—Juvenile fiction. | CYAC:
Palestinian Americans—Fiction. | Grandmothers—Fiction. | Grandparent
and child—Fiction. | Retirement communities—Fiction. | Friendship—
Fiction. |
Florida—Fiction.
Classification: LCC PZ7.1.D3353 Fas 2021 (print) | LCC PZ7.1.D3353
(ebook) | DDC 813.6 [Fic]—dc23
LC record available at https://lccn.loc.gov/2021006160
LC ebook record available at https://lccn.loc.gov/2021006161

Designed by Hilary Wacholz

Farah Rocks
Florida

BY SUSAN
MUADDI DARRAJ

ILLUSTRATED BY
RUAIDA MANNAA

STONE ARCH BOOKS
a capstone imprint

CHAPTER 1

As I stand in front of Harbortown Hospital's large, sliding-glass doors, I hesitate.

"It's okay," Baba urges behind me. He puts his hand on my shoulder. *"Yallah,* Farah," he adds.

I believe him, of course. He's my father, and he'd never tell me to do something that wasn't good for me. (Except maybe for the time I had a bad stomachache, and he told me to eat ice cream because he thought it would cheer me up. Let's just say that my stomach thought it was terrible advice.)

But here's the thing: I think hospitals are nightmare-scary.

I mean, it's a building that is *literally* filled with medicines, needles, and germs.

It's filled with sick people.

And one of them is my little brother.

Baba shifts the cooler to his other hand. When I got home from school today, he was home, packing food for Mama. She's staying at the hospital with Samir. I'm carrying the tall insulated cup Baba uses when he works at the quarry. He filled it with the dark Arabic *qahwah* and stirred in only a tiny amount of sugar "because your mama is already so sweet."

Samir gets sick all the time. We worry a lot about Samir.

He was born very early, like three whole months, and he didn't walk until he was almost four. His lungs did not grow the way they should, and so he has asthma. He also has trouble gripping a pencil because some of his muscles aren't strong yet. He still has trouble pronouncing certain letters, like *r*. When he says my name, it sounds like "Faw-wah."

Last night, he woke up feeling sick. He kept saying, "My hawt, my hawt," touching his palm to his heart in the center of his small chest.

"What does he look like?" I ask Baba now, still hesitating in front of the hospital's doors.

"Like Samir. Silly and funny, just sleepy too."

"Like when he eats too much cake and gets all hyper and then suddenly crashes on the couch?"

"*Sah.*" He smiles halfway, like he's too tired to do it all the way. Baba has a great smile—it stretches along with his mustache across his face. But today, even his mustache looks exhausted. "That's a good way to describe your brother right now."

The hospital doors open wide, then snap shut behind us after we enter.

Everything inside Harbortown Hospital is white and gold. I immediately think about Mount Olympus, where most of the chief gods lived. The floors and walls and desks and chairs and doors are all gleaming-white, like howlite. (That's a pretty white rock. I have a chunk of it in my rock collection at home.) After a second, I realize that the gold is from the sun shining brightly through the lobby's glass skylights. It is reflecting off the white and making everything glitter.

A nurse with a turquoise streak in her blond hair smiles at us. She tells Baba, "Go on up."

"Up," Baba explains on the elevator, is the children's ward. The walls here are bright blue. There's a huge aquarium of colorful fish against one wall, and a mural of butterflies covers another wall. Colorful balloons are anchored to all the nurse's stations, and I feel like maybe we've walked into someone's birthday party by mistake.

"Is this Samir's sister?" asks one nurse, who is wearing a top decorated with emojis.

I nod, noting the bright-red thread woven through her long braids.

"How are you feeling today?" she asks, leaning toward me. "Want to show me?" She indicates the emojis, like options, on her sleeve.

One is smiling, one is laughing, one is crying, one looks scared.

I know what she's doing. I'm in sixth grade at the Magnet Academy, which is a special school for kids like me and Allie Liu, my Official Best Friend. We're called "gifted and talented" (which just means we get more homework than everyone else). I understand that this nurse, with the pretty brown eyes, as dark as Mama's *qahwah*, is trying to help me relax.

Even though it's a trick, I am grateful anyway.

Pointing to the emoji with the panicked, wide eyes, I say, "That's me."

"Understandable. Let's go say hi." She puts her hand on my arm. "Don't be afraid if you see a lot of machines in the room, okay? They're making him better."

As I enter the room, I think, *Here's what she should have said: There will be so many machines, beeping and clicking and blinking, that you may not even know where to find your brother.*

I finally do see him, under a white blanket. He's

huddled like a turtle, with only his black, curly hair sticking out. His right arm hangs out. There is a tube taped down on his skin that connects to a big machine behind him.

He is fast asleep.

"Hi, Farah," says someone else.

Mama.

She sits, holding her rosary beads. Her face is pale, but she looks at me happily.

"I missed you," she says and hugs me.

As I hand her the coffee, she explains that something is wrong with Samir's heart. The nurse adds, "We need to study him for a while to see exactly what is going on."

That sounds good to me. They can keep him here and figure out what is wrong, and then he'll come home. It's only Wednesday. If he comes home tomorrow, we can have Friday night movie night and Saturday morning snuggle-under-the-covers with library books—two of Samir's favorite things to do.

Then Baba says, "Tell her the rest."

Mama sighs and sips her coffee before she speaks. "Farah," she begins, "Samir will be here for at least a week, maybe longer. I have to be with him. When he gets out, I'll have to take care of him at home—we don't know yet how much time he needs to get better. Baba cannot stay home from work another day. He already took off today and tomorrow, and his boss will be mad if he takes more."

"I can stay by myself, or with Allie."

"Listen," Mama says in a big exhale, "I bought you a plane ticket to Florida."

"Wait, what? Florida?" I stop and think hard. "But the only person we know in Florida is . . . is . . . !"

"Farah, please understand . . ."

"Please, no!"

"You're staying with Sitti Fayrouz for a little while."

"How little of a while?" I ask.

"Until everything goes back to normal here."

Holy hummus.

CHAPTER 2

Sometimes adults think they can hide their feelings, but if you pay attention, you can see right through them.

Example: Baba.

He mutters at the car in front of us, which is crawling like a turtle on the freeway. And then, at a red light, he glares at the light like it's causing all his problems.

Translation: He is stressed out.

Before we left the hospital, the nurse said that they would run more tests on Samir tonight. Big Important Tests that will help the doctors decide which other Big

Important Tests need to be done. As we left, I reminded the emoji nurse that Samir is only six, and he weighs about forty-five pounds, so they need to give his body a break. (Mama used to call him *asfour*, or little bird, until he decided he didn't like it.) The nurse nodded and said she would remember.

"You can back your suitcase tonight," Baba says, as the light changes to green. "I will take you tomorrow morning to the airbort." In Arabic, there are no *p*'s and *v*'s, so Baba uses *b*'s instead. You should hear him say "pepperoni pizza."

"Okay," I say, trying to sound like it's no big deal that my family is putting me on a plane, which I have never even been on before, and getting rid of me.

"I'm sorry you have to be away from us for so long," he adds. "But Samir needs time to heal. And Sitti Fayrouz misses you anyway. She is lonely down there and . . . she is very . . . fun."

Fun is not exactly the word I would choose to describe my grandmother, but I stay quiet.

"She likes everything so clean," he says in Arabic and shakes his head. "I remember when I was a boy. . . . You couldn't come in the house if you'd been playing outside. She hates dust and . . ." His voice trails off as he sees my expression in the mirror. Then he smiles sheepishly and changes the subject.

Later that afternoon, I stand in my room with a big suitcase open on my bed. Allie, who's come over to help, hands me shirts from my dresser. I roll them up so they don't wrinkle too much and stack them in the suitcase.

"I remember your grandmother," Allie says. "She was always cooking and sewing."

Sitti Fayrouz lived with us when I was really little. She used to spend the winter in Florida because she said her "old bones" would crack in the Harbortown cold. Then, before Samir was born, she decided she wanted to live in Florida all year long. If we want to see her, we have to go visit her there.

And we have. We drive down a couple of times a year, although we missed last year. I know she's been complaining about that. That explains why my parents are sending me there for a week, or maybe even longer. While they focus on Samir, I'll keep Sitti company so she'll stop complaining about being lonely (even though she is the one who moved in the first place).

"The last time I saw my grandmother," I tell Allie, "she said rocks were dirty and I shouldn't play with them." I sigh. "I tried to tell her I wasn't *playing* with the rocks—I was *studying* them."

"Yeah," she says, handing me socks.

"She has all these *rules*. Everything in her condo has a rule attached to it. I can never keep them straight."

"Like what?"

"Like hang the towel a certain way and brush your hair and tie it up tight in a ponytail so it looks neat. And then she makes me speak Arabic all the time, but I don't speak one hundred percent." Arabic is the other language we speak 1) at home and 2) when Mama doesn't want people to understand us while we're out in public.

"I don't speak Chinese one hundred percent either," Allie says. "It's soooo annoying when people think I should."

"Also, I really don't want to go to Florida," I confess. "I'll miss Samir and my parents and you. I'll even miss my room. I just got used to being in it again."

"I don't like how it happened, but your room is beautiful now," Allie says. We had a house fire a few months ago, and it took a long time to fix it and move back in. My new room is still closet-small, but it's now painted grape-purple (that was the name on the paint can, just so you know). It has a pillow-soft lilac carpet that I love walking on barefoot.

"And," I complain, "I might miss the meetings for the Rock Stars!"

The Rock Stars is the geology festival that Magnet Academy holds every year. The students design exhibits of anything related to rocks and minerals. Then the judges award prizes for the best ones. Allie and I were hoping to make a dynamite presentation.

"It'll be weird not to have Farah Rocks at the meetings," Allie admits. Everyone at school has called me Farah Rocks basically forever. My name is Farah Hajjar, but my last name means "rocks" or "stones" in Arabic. The name has stuck since first grade the way that glitter sticks to everything.

Allie promises me that she will attend the meetings and take lots of notes. "We just have to think of a great idea first," she says.

Baba comes into my room then. "Ms. Maximus from your school is on the phone."

Allie pulls on a thick lock of her black hair, twists it around her finger, and grimaces.

Ms. Maximus's job title is "assistant principal," but she actually controls the whole school. She is also very tough, and she sticks to the rules one hundred percent.

"Well. First of all, I am sorry about your brother. I have no doubt he will be fine." Then she pauses before she says, "Now." That's how I know she's getting serious. "This is a highly unusual situation, Farah," she says. Her voice sounds like when Mama shreds carrots on the grater. "I will have your teachers email all your work to you for the next week. If you end up missing school longer than that, you will do other work virtually. You're also expected to check in frequently with them." Her voice softens just a little. "You *will* get the grades you deserve for the work you do."

"I will get it done," I say, feeling annoyed.

I finish packing, and Allie hugs me before she leaves.

"Wish me luck," I say, hugging her back, hard. "I really need it."

CHAPTER 3

I'm sitting on a small plane, my seat belt cinched glove-tight, in the middle of three seats. A big, white tag hangs from a ribbon around my neck that says "Farah Hajjar—Minor."

Minor means a child, and minors get to board the airplane first. So now I'm waiting while people trudge by me, bonking their bags down the aisle while looking for their seat number. Bored, I remove the paper tag from its plastic case and use my black pen to insert *tau* after the *o* in *minor*.

The lady who helped me board sees me return the tag to the plastic case. "What are you doing?" She's wearing a navy blue uniform, and her makeup looks thick, like she painted it on her face with a brush.

"Decorating my tag."

Bending down, she reads, "*Minotaur*. What does that mean?"

"Just a character I like from Greek mythology. Actually, I feel kind of sad for him."

"Why?" she asks with a tight smile.

"He's trapped in a labyrinth," I explain. "Isn't that awful?"

"A what?" She stands tall again and scrunches her eyebrows at me. "Look, honey, just don't tamper with your tag."

She moves away, down the aisle, and I sigh, looking around me as other people continue boarding. It's my first time on an airplane. Attached to the back of the seat is a tray that folds down, like a little table. But I can't open it, the lady said, until after the plane is in the air.

I brought my colored pencils and my red notebook, so that I can do some drawing during the flight.

When we've visited Sitti in Florida in the past, my father drove us in our car, and we slept in a small hotel along the way. It takes ten hours. This plane ride, according to my ticket, should take only one hour and forty-two minutes. That is amazing to me! There are seven hundred miles to cover, so I try to calculate how fast the plane must be flying.

As people keep entering the plane, Uniform Lady greets each one cheerfully. "Welcome! So glad to have you with us today."

"Do you want the window, sweetie?" asks a lady who has stopped in my aisle. She wears a big, blue straw hat on her head. "I don't mind."

"Thank you!" I say happily because I didn't even know you were *allowed* to change seats. I thought it was like school, where you have an assigned seat and that's that.

I unbuckle and scoot over, pushing up the window

shade to look at the airport runway. Mama told me I will be able to see the clouds when we're up in the air.

Blue Hat sits down beside me. "Can't wait to get home," she says, shoving her big purse under the seat in front of her. Sitting up straight again, she asks, "You're awfully brave to be traveling by yourself."

"I'm visiting my grandmother."

"That's sweet," she says. "Wish my grandson would come and see me, but he never has."

"Do you have a lot of rules in your house?" I ask, trying to be helpful. "If you have too many, that might be why. Just my opinion."

She looks startled, then thoughtful. "I have *some* rules. I'll think on that now."

Just then, a man towers over us, looking annoyed. "I have the window seat," he says sharply. His eyes are staring at the row of storage bins above our heads.

"It was my seat, sir, and I gave it to this young lady."

Blue Hat pulls out her ticket and shows him, but he barely looks at it. Instead he beckons over Uniform Lady and tells her, "Window seat's mine."

Uniform Lady examines both tickets. "It's technically his seat," she explains to Blue Hat. "Your seat is the aisle, not the window."

"Can I still have the window?" I ask the man politely. "I want to draw the clouds."

Uniform Lady and Blue Hat swivel their heads toward him, smiling, like they're about to witness a kind act.

Instead, he glares at me and acid-hisses, "No."

Holy hummus.

Blue Hat gasps. "I'm sorry for the mix-up," she whispers to me. "My goodness."

We have to all stand up and move into the aisle so the man can squeeze in. He buckles his seat belt, pulls his black hat down over his face, and goes to sleep.

Blue Hat offers to take the center seat. "So you don't have to sit next to this grouch," she whispers.

"I heard you," he mutters. Then, with his eyes still closed, he reaches out and pulls down the window shade. Now there's no way I'll see the clouds.

From my aisle seat, I lean forward and look around Blue Hat to study the man closely. He is wearing a green cotton shirt stamped with pictures of big, white flowers. He is grandfather-old, and he has no hair on his head. But if he did, it would be Santa-white, like his bushy eyebrows.

He frowns even while he's sleeping.

As we take off, Blue Hat gives me some chewing gum to help my ears not hurt from the pressure. I'm not sure how it works exactly, but it's a good trick, and it helps. Halfway through the flight, Uniform Lady marches down the aisle with a cart, serving drinks. She gets to me and asks, "Beverage?"

I wish I could get a soda, but I don't have any money on me. I wish Baba had remembered to give me a few dollars, but he was rushing.

"No, thank you."

Blue Hat asks for a Coke. When I don't see her hand over any money, I whisper to her, "Wait, is it free?"

"Yes," she explains. "I was surprised you didn't want one."

"Wow, it's *free*?" I say again. I turn back to Uniform Lady. "Excuse me, but can I get an orange soda?" I yelp. Then I lower my voice: "Please."

Grinning, she hands me the drink, which I place carefully on my tray. She also gives me a pack of pretzels. They must also be free!

She glances at the Grouch near the window. "Not waking him up," she says under her breath and gets ready to move on.

"But maybe he wants a drink," I say.

"No, I'd better not," she mutters and starts to move down the aisle.

Suddenly I feel bad for him. If I'd fallen asleep and missed out on a free orange soda, I'd be pretty upset. So I reach over Blue Hat and tap him on the arm. "Sir? Wake up, sir!"

He jumps up, startled, and his arm juts out, knocking over the Coke on Blue Hat's tray. She tries to grab it, but it tips back. And then they're both shrieking because the Coke spills onto his lap. It soaks his tan shorts and drips down his legs.

"WHAT!?" he barks.

"Holy hummus," I manage to squeak.

He glares at me. "Did you . . . did you actually *poke* me?" he growls.

"Now, calm down, sir," says Blue Hat. She hands him her napkin. "She just wanted to see if you'd like a drink."

"Even if I did, I wouldn't want it all over my LAP!"

"But they're free," I offer.

"*Of course* they're free. They're *always* free." He hisses something I can't hear while Uniform Lady also hands him a stack of napkins. All around us, people are peering over their seats to stare.

"Who lets a kid fly by herself?" he mumbles. "It's like they let a horse loose on this plane."

"Did you just call me a . . . a horse?" I ask in shock, because now I am getting pretty mad.

He glares at me again, then notices my white tag. "Guess I was wrong. They've actually unleashed a Minotaur."

CHAPTER 4

The plane lands in St. Augustine, touching down on the runway exactly one hour and forty-seven minutes after we took off. (They shouldn't call it "touching down" when it feels more like the plane is smacking the asphalt and all the bones in your body shake.)

Uniform Lady tells me to wait until everyone else leaves, and then she will walk me out.

"Have fun in Florida," says Blue Hat. She pulls her big purse out and stands up. She has to hunch over because the overhead bins are so low. I scoot out into the aisle to make room for her.

"I hope your grandson visits you soon."

"So do I," she says and pats me on the head. Then she hands me a package. "I saved my pretzels for you." She giggles at the excited, goofy look on my face.

The Grouch follows her, ignoring me. The front of his pants is still soaked, and when he walks up the aisle, I see there is a big, damp patch on the back of his shorts too. I almost laugh, because it looks like he wet his pants, but I bite my lips shut tight.

I sit and wait while everyone shuffles back past me, lugging their bags again. When the aisle is finally clear, Uniform Lady crooks her finger at me. We walk together up the walkway that looks like a jagged, carpeted hallway. I realize it is a movable plank that connects the airplane's door to the airport.

It makes sense because I am about to spend at least a week with Sitti—it really *does* feel like I'm walking the plank!

When we enter the actual airport, Uniform Lady makes me wait until she can walk me out of the terminal. That's the part of the airport we're in. Finally, she's ready and we walk down a long hallway, where they have escalators that stay flat on the ground. They're like rides you hop on to walk even faster.

When we pass through a big set of doors, I see Sitti immediately. She is wearing a long, black *thobe* with red and white embroidery on it. She embroiders these dresses herself. Her hair is partly covered with a loose, white veil.

She's holding a sign that says *Farah Hajjar.*

Just so you know, she's tiny, like a little fairy.

"I need to see your ID," Uniform Lady says to Sitti.

But Sitti ignores her and reaches up, planting one hand on each side of my face. She pulls my face down and kisses me four times on each cheek and then once on the forehead. With each kiss, she pushes my head away and then back in, like she thinks my neck is made out of rubber.

"Umm . . . ," says Uniform Lady, "I need to get back to work so . . . your ID?"

Sitti looks at me in confusion. "What does she want?" she asks me in Arabic.

Holy hummus. I think of the Arabic words to translate for her. "She needs . . . She wants to see your . . . your . . ." What's the word for *ID*? I settle on *waraq*, which just means "paper."

"What paper?"

Holy hummus.

"Your driver's paper?" I try again in Arabic. I don't know the word for *ID*.

"I don't drive. I took the shuttle from the condo." Sitti looks annoyed with *me* now. "By the way, your Arabic is terrible."

Ah, yes, I think. *It's going to be a week or more of constant, annoying reminders that I can understand more Arabic than I can actually speak.*

Finally, Uniform Lady pulls out her own airline ID, a plastic card with her photo on it.

"Do you have any ID?" she says slowly and loudly.

"Tell her I can hear," Sitti grumbles, but she understands now. She reaches her hand into the front of her dress. My face turns red as I see Uniform Lady's eyebrows shoot up.

I know what she's doing: There is a hidden pocket that she reaches from the side, under her arm. But it still looks funny. A second later, Sitti pulls out a fat wallet, so stuffed that the leather is creased and the little clasp barely closes.

Flipping it open, she shows the lady a photograph on a card that reads *Grand Palms Independent Living Association*, and her name, *Fayrouz Hanna Hajjar.*

"Izz good?" she asks the lady in stumbling English. When she nods, Sitti closes the wallet and replaces it in the front of her dress.

I can't help but wonder what else she has in there.

Sitti takes my hand like I am two years old and pulls me toward the baggage claim area. I try to take my hand back, but she is really strong for a small, old person.

I find my bag easily, because Baba tied a thick, red ribbon around the handle. Sitti tells me in Arabic, "Hurry up, or we will miss the shuttle."

A shuttle bus sits right outside the baggage area. The side of the shuttle is painted with palm trees and, in curly pink type, reads Grand Palms.

"Grand Palms? That isn't where you lived before," I say, not recognizing the name.

"No, I moved," she says. "This place is better— Grand Bums!"

I make sure I don't laugh at how she pronounces Palms, but it's just so funny I have to smile.

The driver is standing beside the door, smiling and helping people with their bags. "Is this your granddaughter?" he asks Sitti, and she nods and points to me. He takes my bag and announces, "I'm Mr. Delacroix, here to help." He has a nice accent, soft and gentle as a butterfly, not heavy like my grandmother's.

"Nice to meet you, sir," I say.

"Hop on. We only have one other passenger today."

He takes my bag around to the back of the shuttle, and I follow Sitti up the short steps into the vehicle. I glance into the driver's seat and see that books are scattered everywhere. They're stuffed on the dashboard and piled on the passenger seat next to him.

I'm trying to squint and read some of the titles when, in front of me, Sitti stiffens and mutters in Arabic, "Oh no, not him."

I look past her, which is easy because I can see right over her head.

There, sleeping in a seat by the window, is the last person I wanted to see.

It's the Grouch.

I'm so shocked, I say nothing. Sitti whispers to me in Arabic, "A miserable old man. He hates everyone."

"He was on the plane with me." I try to find the Arabic word for *rude*, but my brain is not telling me.

"Look," she says in a huff, "his pants. He's probably wet himself."

CHAPTER 5

During the short ride, Sitti asks me four million questions. I don't know enough words to tell her more than that Samir is fine and Mama is fine and Baba is fine and school is fine and the house is fine.

A few minutes later, Mr. Delacroix calls out, "We've arrived!"

The condos of Grand Palms are laid out in several large buildings that remind me of taffy—pink, pale blue, creamy yellow, mint green. There is so much color that I want to take my pencils out of my backpack and draw everything I see: the benches sprinkled around the green lawn, the tall palms that are clustered everywhere, the pathway that leads back to a pond, and beyond that, some trees.

The taffy buildings form a half circle, and in the middle is another, shorter one that looks like it's made completely of glass. Sitti tells me it's called the Hub, where the main lobby and dining hall are. It's a gathering place for all the residents.

The Grouch sits up in his seat and yawns. "We here?" he asks the driver.

"Sure are, Dr. Fisher," the driver calls back. "Home sweet home."

Dr. Fisher looks around him and spots Sitti.

"Fay," he says gruffly. She sniffs at him and looks out the window.

Then he spots me, and his mouth drops open. The way he looks reminds me of his name in that second; he looks like a big fish. A fish that's just been pulled out of the water and is trying to catch its breath. His head wiggles around, and his mouth opens and closes without a sound.

"Hi," I say. Then I add, "Remember me? The Minotaur?"

"How could I forget?" he mutters.

. . .

Everyone at Grand Palms is old.

Ancient-old.

But they're super-friendly.

Unlike Dr. Fisher, who stalks off to the elevators, everyone in the lobby smiles at me and says hi. I feel like a little kitten that they all want to pet. One lady with a long, flowery dress and a walking cane even pats my head. Another man, who is wearing shorts and tan socks pulled up to his knees, peers at me and asks where I live.

"Harbortown," I say.

"Oooh . . . so cold up there," he says with a shiver. "It's much nicer down here, warm and sunny. Right, Fay?"

She looks at him in confusion.

"Sunny here in Florida, right?"

Understanding, she nods, smiling. "Yes, izz so good, good for zee bones."

"Everyone adores your grandmother," the man tells me. "She's very special to us. I'm Don Mitchell. Call me Mitch."

"And I'm Agatha," says the lady with the flowery dress, patting me on the head again.

Sitti's condo is on the first floor, past the lobby. On the door hangs a sign that reads *Mrs. Fayrouz Hajjar*, in embroidered red thread on a black fabric square.

Inside, there is a small kitchen and a big living room with teal-colored fabric couches. I see a fireplace in the living room, although I'm not sure why you would need one of those in Florida. The floor is covered with plastic runners to protect the white carpet.

A narrow hallway leads to several other doors, which I guess are the bedrooms and the bathroom. All the walls are lemon-yellow, and there are embroidered pillows everywhere.

Literally everywhere. I *do* remember this from our last visit.

The couches each have ten pillows on them, lined up like little candy squares. There are larger pillows piled up on a rug on the floor, next to the fireplace. Each of the kitchen chairs, lined up under a short counter, has an embroidered cushion on the seat.

I start to walk down the hallway, but Sitti yelps at me to come back and take off my shoes. I do this at home, just so you know. I just forgot.

She makes a huge deal about how I need to line up my shoes on the plastic tray she keeps in her foyer and how I always have to hang up my jacket *immediately* in the hall closet. "And if your hands are dirty, you go wash them right away before you touch the furniture or the walls or *anything*," she says, pointing up at me with her index finger, like she is stabbing the air.

"Yes, yes," I mumble, then continue to investigate. Down the hallway, I peek inside a door—the bathroom. Even the small towel's borders are embroidered with blue flowers.

I peek inside the bedroom she says is mine. It's small, and there is only a tiny nightstand and a narrow bed. A large, soft blanket covers the bed, embroidered with an outline of a big, gray bird. It has a black head and a patch of yellow near its tail. And of course, the bed is also covered with lots of pillows—about eight of them, all piled up near the headboard.

"Did you embroider all these, Sitti?" I ask her in Arabic.

She shrugs and replies, "I have time for *tatreez*."

It looks to me like she has a *lot* of time.

"Come, let's eat," she says. "I have the food ready."

We head back to the kitchen. I sit at the counter, on one of the cushioned seats.

She goes to the oven, to the large pots and a pan filled with sautéed pine nuts—*magloubeh*, one of my favorite foods. It's rice cooked with cauliflower and chicken and potatoes, and topped with pine nuts (even though sometimes Mama skips the chicken when we are short on money).

"Here," Sitti says. She puts a heap on a plate and then sprinkles pine nuts over the whole thing.

I eat like I have never tasted food before while Sitti just keeps adding more scoops of *magloubeh*. "More, more," she says in Arabic, pinching my arm. "You're too skinny."

"I'm not skinny," I say. Except I have a mouthful of *magloubeh*, so it sounds like "Arh nom shinny."

There is a knock on the door, and when Sitti calls, "Come!" Mr. Delacroix strides in, pulling my suitcase behind him.

"Your bag, young lady," he says, grinning.

"Thank you," Sitti says, except it sounds like "Think you," and she starts fixing another plate. "You eat?"

He sits down at the counter beside me. "Fay, I will never say no to your food." He looks at me and laughs because my mouth is still full.

Sitti points to him and tells me, "He a-from Haiti, but hizz English more zan mine."

Mr. Delacroix laughs and says, "It takes time, Fay." I don't tell him she has been in the United States for longer than I have been alive. I really do like his accent, like a whisper that floats in the air after the word.

"How's your brother?" he asks me politely. I suddenly realize everyone at Grand Bums, as Sitti calls it, must know why I have come here.

I tell him that Samir is having a bunch of tests and probably surgery soon.

"I hope he will be all right. I'm sure he will be," and he says it so confidently that I believe him. "Also," he adds, leaning toward me, "sorry about the reception you got from Dr. Fisher."

"He was actually on the plane with me too." I swallow my food then confess, "I accidentally dumped a cold soda on his lap."

Mr. Delacroix starts laughing so hard that I'm afraid the rice is going to shoot out of his nose. (That's possible, just so you know—I saw it happen to Samir once.) When he stops laughing, he says, "I wondered what had happened to his pants! I thought . . . well, you know." He laughed again. "He is a strange man. Cranky. Always has been."

"He's pretty old," I say, which makes Mr. Delacroix grin again. "What kind of doctor is he?"

"Something to do with environmental science." Mr. Delacroix shrugs. "We all avoid him, mostly because . . ." He pauses, then looks at me uncertainly.

"What? Why?" I put my hands together like a prayer. "Please tell me!"

"Nothing. He's just unusual."

"Unusual how?" I'm not letting it drop.

His voice gets really low. "Once I went into his condo

because he had a large package delivered, and he was away for a trip. And in there, I found . . ."

"What?"

"Well, maybe I shouldn't say . . ."

"Holy hummus, what?"

"Skulls. Skulls, everywhere."

CHAPTER 6

Later that afternoon, I actually fall asleep on one of Sitti's couches, because I ate more than I usually do in a week.

I hear someone call my name, then Sitti nudges me awake. She hands me her cell phone, saying, "Your mother."

"Mama!" I say excitedly into the phone.

"How was your flight?" she asks.

I tell her all about Uniform Lady and Blue Hat and Dr. Fisher, who ended up being Sitti's grouchy neighbor. I don't mention the stuff about the skulls. (I thought Mr. Delacroix had been joking with me earlier, but he promised, before he left, that he was standardized-test serious.)

"How's Samir?" I ask.

She tells me that they know what is wrong with his heart. "It's called a ventricular septal defect, or VSD," she explains. It's like an opening in the tissues between the chambers of his heart. "So his heart has to work harder, and this is why it can be dangerous. He's actually had this for a long time, Farah. It was supposed to close up by now, but it has not."

"So . . . it's like . . . a hole in his heart?"

"Basically, yes." I hear her swallow loudly on the other end. When I hear that deep gulp and then her shaky breath, I feel my own throat tighten up.

"Can they fix it?" I manage to ask, but before I finish the question, I know it is silly. As if you can sew up a hole in someone's heart like Mama sews up the knees of Samir's pants. Or pack the hole full of Play-Doh like I did once when I pulled a nail out of my bedroom wall and it left a big gash.

"He will need surgery," she says quietly.

My stomach clenches up, and I hope I am not about to hurl all the *magloubeh* I just ate.

"Farah?" she says. "They do these surgeries all the time, *habibti*. They will take care of him. I don't want you to worry."

I say okay, because I know that she doesn't need to worry about me too. I even stay quiet and don't get mad when she says it looks like I will need to stay in Florida for a few weeks for sure. And I promise her I will listen to Sitti and work on my schoolwork and be on my best behavior. She promises to call me every day.

Then I hang up the phone and lie down on the couch again, resting my palm on my chest until I can feel the beat, right in the center. I focus on the rhythm, steady and strong, and I wonder what it must feel like to have a hole in your heart.

. . .

On Saturday mornings, the residents at Grand Bums eat breakfast together. Sitti says she doesn't usually go, but Mr. Delacroix knocks on her door and insists she come down. "So your granddaughter can meet everyone," he says.

"I do food here," she mumbles, pulling her veil forward on her forehead. It keeps slipping down all the time.

"No, no! Fay, you need to come and hang out with everyone else," he insists and points his finger at me. "Come on, young lady. They're all dying to meet you."

I have been checking the emails from my teachers and thinking about the Rock Stars fair, trying to form an idea. My brain hurts, and I'm ready to get out of the condo.

Everywhere I look, the dining hall is decorated with flowers. Every table has a vase of flowers, and the wallpaper is covered in yellow daisies. The curtains on the big window also have flowers on the borders. Someone went crazy in here with the flower decorations, the way Sitti did with her embroidery in her condo.

People are clustered around the tables. A group of them beckon Sitti over. She shuffles toward them in her long dress. I recognize Mitch and Agatha, and I introduce myself to several others.

Sitti reaches into the front of her dress and pulls out a plastic card. "Use this to go and buy something to eat," she says to me in Arabic. She points to the food counter that is in the other room.

"Can I get a soda?" I ask.

She nods, but only because I don't think she knows what *soda* means.

Just as I am about to clap in glee, Mitch says, "At nine a.m.? Fay, is that a good idea?" When Sitti doesn't answer, he looks at me and waggles his finger. "Shouldn't have sugar so early, young lady. Now get something healthy and come tell us all about yourself."

I smile politely, even though I want to throw a thunderbolt like Zeus. At the buffet line, I fill a plate with scrambled eggs and two pancakes. There are glasses of orange juice, so I place one on my tray. Everyone is friendly—the servers, the cashier, even the cook comes out from behind the window to say hi to "Fay's granddaughter, from out of state."

"Your grandmother doesn't talk much, but she is a sweet lady," the cook says. He is tall and thinner than a spaghetti noodle, with a short, red beard. When he smiles, his grin fills up the whole bottom half of his face.

"Thank you!" I say awkwardly, as if I somehow made Sitti the way she is.

"My name's Bill McCallum, but you can call me Cal," he says.

I think it's pretty neat how most people here get their name shortened: Fay, Mitch, Cal. "Thanks, Mr. Cal," I say. "I'm Farah—"

A gruff voice comes from behind me. "Are you going to move, Minotaur, or just hold up the line?"

Holy hummus.

"Morning, Dr. Fisher," says Cal, though I notice his

voice becomes suddenly church-serious. "Did you meet Fay's granddaugh—"

"Yes, yes, unfortunately, I did." He picks up a plate of bacon from the counter and moves past me. "I don't have all day." He walks up to the cashier, scans his card in the machine, and stalks away.

"Don't let him bother you, not one bit," says Cal, but he still doesn't bring back his amazing smile. "He's just a mean old . . . err . . ."

"Grouch?" I offer. "Crank? Meanie?"

"All of those." The cook shakes his head. "Well, you won't see him much anyway. He spends all of his time back in the woods, near the pond, doing who-knows-what."

"He used to be nice," says the cashier, a woman about the same age as my mom. "Before."

"Before what?" I ask.

But she won't say. Instead, she wishes me a good day and serves the people in line behind me.

"Farah, your grandmother tells us that you are quite

the brilliant student," says Mitch when I return to the table. "What grade are you in?"

"I tell dem you smart," Sitti says in her cute English.

And in between bites of my scrambled eggs (which are the best I've ever had), I tell them all about the Magnet Academy, about my Official Best Friend, Allie Liu, about the writing club I started at school earlier this year, and about the upcoming Rock Stars fair.

"What will you present at the fair?" Agatha asks me.

I shrug. "No clue. I think someone else is already doing something about erosion. Another team is doing something on lava rocks, which would have been cool."

Sitti pokes me in the arm, and I know she wants me to translate for her, but I'm honestly not sure how to say *lava rocks* in Arabic. Looking annoyed because I am stumbling over my Arabic words, she gets up and comes back with a cup of tea. She reaches into the front of her thobe again and pulls out a Ziploc bag with peppermint leaves in it. She pulls out two long leaves and drops them into her paper teacup, then returns the bag to her dress.

Holy hummus.

I am embarrassed and look around at everyone else, but they don't seem to notice that my grandmother is pulling actual food out of her clothes.

"Well, maybe you will think of something while you're here," says Mitch kindly. "Everyone here would be happy to help." He frowns as Dr. Fisher walks by our table, dumps his tray into the trash can, and walks outside. "Well, maybe not everyone."

CHAPTER 7

One day, Sitti wakes me early to go to the chapel. There is no church close by where they speak Arabic, she says, so the chapel is good enough. We get dressed and walk to the Grand Bums clubhouse. It has three main sections: the chapel, a gym, and a pool. I imagine people getting up from praying and then diving into a pool, which makes me snicker until Sitti shushes me.

"Be respectful," she says in Arabic.

We push open the wooden door and enter the quiet space. Three rows of pews line both sides. On a long table at the front, candles sit in a large bowl of sand. The wax drips like tears down the slim candlesticks.

We walk to the front, and Sitti picks up a candle. "Let's light one for Samir," she says.

Tears rush up into my eyes like a hot wave, and I blink really hard so they don't run down my cheeks. I'm nightmare-scared about doctors operating on my brother's tiny heart.

But I light the candle without saying a thing, and then Sitti takes my hand and pulls me, like she did at the airport, to a pew. Sitti has a rosary, and she says a prayer in Arabic for every bead. When she finishes the prayer, she grips the next bead between her thumb and index finger and repeats it. There is something about her voice, about the repetition, that makes me feel quiet inside. I decide that I like the peace of it all.

Half an hour later, we leave and go back to her condo. I sit down and look through my homework again. I'm working on a worksheet about square roots when I hear a phone ring.

I look around but don't see the phone. Then I notice Sitti reaching inside her dress.

Yes. She does it.

She pulls a cell phone out of her clothes.

One day, I think, *she is going to be like a magician and pull a rabbit out of there.*

"Yes?" she says as she answers, then she launches into a stream of Arabic: "How are you? Good to hear your voice. Yes, thank goodness, I am fine. Yes, she is staying with me for a while. Who told you that? Oh, how is she doing . . . ?"

I finish my square roots sheet. Because she is still talking, I snuggle up on the couch, hugging a big embroidered pillow to my chest. There is a small basket behind the pillow, and I take it out. Inside, there is a square of black fabric and several small balls of thread, with needles stuck in them as if they're pincushions.

I open the square and see the outline of a bird.

"It's a *bulbul*," Sitti says, as she closes her cell phone.

I like the way it sounds: *bulbul*, like a little poem. She explains to me that it's a songbird back home in Palestine.

"It's the same bird as on the blanket on the bed," I tell her.

"It's our village symbol," she says but then smiles when I look confused.

"Did you ever look at my thobes closely?" she asks.

I look carefully at the one she wears today. It's made of green fabric with yellow embroidery, and there it is, a *bulbul*, embroidered along the sleeves and the hemline.

"Every village back home has a symbol we use in our *tatreez*," she explains. "*Tatreez* is part of our culture." She points to her dress. "Some villages have certain flowers, like roses or lilies, or specific birds, or religious symbols." She plucks the fabric square from my hand and threads a needle as she explains. "Anyone who sees me can tell which village I am from just by the designs on my dress."

"It's like a . . ." I struggle to find the word. Then it

pops into my head. "Like a code," I tell her, and she nods thoughtfully, like it makes sense.

She finds an extra square of fabric in her basket. "Come on," she says. "I will teach you *tatreez*, just like I learned when I was your age."

At first, I'm excited, but then five minutes later, I realize something: *Tatreez is hard.*

It takes me forever just to learn how to thread the needle. I close one eye to do it, but still stick my finger at least three times.

Something else: *Tatreez* requires math! I have to count the number of stitches I need to make and then make sure I have the space on the fabric to do so. The fabric is divided into little squared cells, and I have to calculate how many squares I will need to match the design. Sitti can do these calculations super quickly in her head.

When I stick my finger yet again, she makes a noise with her mouth, like she is hitting her tongue against the back of her teeth. *She's like a rattlesnake,* I think, as she snatches the fabric from my hand.

"Enough," she says with a huff, folding it up. "We'll try again tomorrow. Go make your bed, please. You forgot to do it this morning."

After I make my bed, I decide to walk around Grand Bums on my own. Sitti gives me a key to her condo and a paper map that she pulls out of a kitchen drawer.

First I go to the recreation center. The gym is interesting, because it is filled with people, but nobody seems to be doing any exercise. One man stands on the treadmill, chatting with an old lady who is sitting and not biking on the stationary bicycle. Two other ladies are sitting on a floor mat, with their legs extended, but they are not bending, just talking and laughing.

But then I see Dr. Fisher, over on the side. He is on the ground, doing push-ups, and holy hummus, he is really moving. Up and down, up and down. I am surprised by how strong he is for an old man. I remember what Mr. Delacroix told me about the skulls, and I move on before he finishes and sees me watching him.

Next, I go outside and take the path I saw on the first day, strolling toward the pond. It's filled with ducks, quacking like they are a music band. Mr. Delacroix drives by in the shuttle and pauses, calling to me from the window. "Hey, Farah! Go inside and get some old bread from the kitchen to feed them."

"Good idea!" I say, then hurry in and ask Cal. He looks like he is crying because his eyes are as red as his hair.

"I'm okay . . . just chopping onions," he reassures me with a smile, pointing to the neat piles of onions on his cutting board. "Ducks can't eat bread—I save the vegetable scraps for them." He hands me a small bag filled with shards of celery and carrot leaves and tells me to have fun.

The first time I throw a small sliver of celery, a flock of ducks attacks it. A tall one with brown feathers snatches the morsel. The others, who are hungry and now know there is food nearby, turn and—in one yellow and white wave—waddle toward me in a stampede! I back up, tossing scraps at them as fast as I can rip them out of the bag. After a few minutes, they calm down, maybe knowing there is enough food to go around. I calm down too, knowing I won't be trampled by these feathered, quacking monsters.

When my scraps are gone, I head down the path again, toward the tall palm trees and thick, mossy grass. I push through one area, scanning the ground for interesting rocks. My rock collection at home is pretty large. Luckily, Baba works at a quarry, so he always brings home interesting stones for me.

I wonder if I can add something from this trip to my collection, although I will have to sneak them by Sitti Fayrouz. The other day, I found a grasshopper on the lawn and trapped him in a paper cup. I was going to bring him inside to try to draw him, but Sitti made me release him. "No bugs in the house!" she practically shrieked. "I have rules, and you have to follow them."

Doesn't she know she has

more rules than the whole United States government?

Near a bush of wildflowers, I find some white stones that I don't recognize. I put them in my pocket. Farther along, I find flat gray shards. But after looking at them closely, I realize they are just chunks of cement, so I put them back, disappointed. Even farther, I find one pretty pink stone with layers in it. I keep that too.

And then, under a palm tree, I pick up a brown and red stone that looks oddly like a chunk of tree bark. I find more like it, and then I kneel down and start digging. The dirt is getting under my nails. I know Sitti will be annoyed, but I keep going because I have a hunch.

And I'm right. About two inches down in the brown dirt, I find a whole cluster of these strange rocks.

I pick one up and hold it up to the sunlight. It glistens with streaks of red and blue, as if little crystals are embedded in it. Even though Sitti will be mad, I stuff a few into my pockets.

Suddenly, there's that gruff voice again. "What are you doing here?"

I look over my shoulder and see Dr. Fisher.

He's scary enough, but now there's something even scarier about him.

In his right hand, he is holding a tiny, white skull.

"Holy hummus!" I shriek, then jump up and run like lightning back to Grand Bums.

CHAPTER 8

Sitti is napping on the sofa. My heart is still hammering from seeing Dr. Fisher with a skull. I have to tell Mr. Delacroix he was right about that. While Sitti dozes, I sneak the rocks out of my pockets and run them under water in the bathroom sink. Then I wrap them in a towel and put them under my bed.

I go on the Internet to see if I can find anything about the new rock I discovered, but there is nothing. I don't even know what search terms to use.

When Sitti wakes up, she asks me if I want to take a turn cooking something tonight for dinner.

"I don't know how to cook," I tell her.

She stares at me.

"I can make sandwiches, but not anything that has to be cooked on a stove."

Her mouth hangs open in surprise. Then she shakes her head: "Can't embroider. Can't cook. Can barely speak Arabic."

She throws up her hands and tells me she's taking the shuttle to go grocery shopping. Now, I'm annoyed with her for sure, so I say that I'm staying behind to do my schoolwork and call my parents. The truth is that I don't want to be around her right now.

Sitti leaves me her cell phone, and I call my parents.

"Samir is okay," Mama says after she answers the phone. "Want to talk to him?" Of course I do, because I haven't really heard his voice since that night when he woke up sick.

"Hi, Faw-wah," he says in a whisper-soft voice. His voice is low. He sounds nothing like my brother, who is always a huge wave of energy and fun.

"How are you feeling?"

"Sleepy," he says. "But guess what? I have a TV in my woom."

He tells me that the Lius came to visit him, and they brought food for Mama and a Tommy Turtle DVD collection for him. That's been his favorite cartoon character basically since he was born.

Later, Mama comes back on the phone and tells me that his surgery for VSD is set for two days from now. "They're waiting until he gets a little stronger. They want him to be ready," she says. "He will be fine, *inshallah*," she says calmly. "How are things going with Sitti?"

Here's what I want to say: *She loves me. I know that. But she's bossy. She thinks I don't know how to do anything. And she cleans all day even when there is nothing to clean.*

Here's what I actually say: "Great, Mama. Everything is great."

. . .

My teachers at the Magnet Academy prepared packets of homework and sheets for me to complete while I am in Florida. For a language arts assignment, I need to look up *Spartu* online in the student encyclopedia. But instead, I do what I have been doing almost every day: I Google *VSD*.

The websites all have the same basic information:

VSD is a common type of heart defect, often found among prematurely born children. It is a hole in the wall that separates the two lower chambers of the heart. It often requires surgery to be repaired.

So much for focusing on Sparta.

I pick up Sitti's embroidery instead and try to work on my stitches. Cross over and then back around to form the *x*, like she taught me.

I wish I could take my thread and stitch up the hole in Samir's heart myself. That would make everything all right again.

Because Sitti is still not back, I take the embroidery and head down to the dining hall. It is empty except for

Cal, who is preparing dinner. He passes me an orange soda. I try to give him Sitti's plastic card so he can charge me, but he just waves me off.

"Thank you!" I say.

"You're welcome," he says, giving me his huge smile. "It's nice for all these old folks to have a young person around."

I sit by the big fountain and work on my cross-stitch. I place Sitti's piece, the picture of the *bulbul*, in front of me to use as a model.

Suddenly someone behind me says, "Why are you stitching a *Passeriforme*?"

It's Dr. Fisher, and I look around wildly to see where Cal went. Of course, he's nowhere to be seen.

I'm alone with the Grouch.

The Grouch who collects skulls.

I look back at the old man, standing there, with his hands in his shorts pockets. His shirt is like the one he wore on the plane—cotton, with buttons down the front and big, green palm leaves stamped all over it.

"It's a *bulbul*," I say. It sounds like I am squeaking.

"Speak up, girl," he barks. "What did you say?"

"It's a *bulbul*," I repeat.

"Ah . . . ," he says, pausing. "Yes, a *Pycnonotus xanthopygos.*"

"A what?" I ask, staring at him.

"A white-spectacled *bulbul*. It's known for that yellow vent."

"What's a . . . a vent?" Now I'm curious.

"It's that patch on its . . . well, on its backside."

And then he does something I completely don't expect.

He blushes.

The Grouch from the airplane actually *blushes.*

"*Backside* is not a bad word, just so you know," I tell him kindly because maybe when he was a little kid, a long, long time ago, it was.

"Well, thanks for that." He examines my stitching. "I didn't know that Minotaurs can embroider. Is Fay teaching you?"

I nod. "I'm not very good yet."

"No," he agrees, "you're not."

I blink because I cannot believe that he is so rude! But I'm starting to think that this is just his personality. "Well, there's a lot of counting," I explain. "And sometimes I mess up."

"You will improve." He says it like a command. Not like, *Don't worry, you will get better,* but, *Hey you! You WILL do better.* Then he gives me a strange look. "Why did you scream when you saw me earlier?"

I really wish Cal would walk by now. Right now would be a good time.

"It was just an odd reaction," he continues, "don't you think? I mean, I know we don't have a lot in common. You're a Minotaur and I'm a human, but isn't screaming a little dramatic?"

Holy hummus, did he just make a joke? I wonder. I think he did, and that gives me the courage to be honest with him.

"Well, maybe it's because you were walking around

carrying a skull," I say hesitantly and lift up my shoulders. "Like, who does that?"

"I am a *scientist*," he says, sniffing the air as if there is a bad odor suddenly. "And specifically, I am an *ornithologist*. Do you know what that is?"

"Nope."

"A scientist who studies birds. I collect the remains of birds—their bones, their skulls—when I find them."

"Okay."

He bends down until he is looking me right in the eye. "They are already dead when I find them," he says, as if to make sure I understand.

"That's . . . good to know," I say. He kind of snickers, as if he liked my joke. Except that I wasn't joking.

"And what were *you* doing in the woods?" he asks.

I tell him about the strange rocks I found. He tells me to bring them down to breakfast one day so he can examine them.

Then, without even saying goodbye, he turns and walks out the door.

"You okay, there?" asks Cal, who appears suddenly, carrying a huge sack of rice over his shoulder.

"I think so." I watch Dr. Fisher's tall form, heading out toward the pond at Grand Bums.

"He's a strange man," says Cal.

Yesterday, I would have agreed.

Today seems different.

Today, I think maybe Dr. Fisher is just a lonely, sad person.

CHAPTER 9

Allie calls me the next day to tell me all the news from the Magnet Academy.

Our friend Brian Najjarian got picked to go on a special field trip to Washington, D.C., to visit some of the Smithsonian museums.

June Jordan, our friend from writing club, wrote a new poem that is being printed in the school's newsletter.

And Enrique LeBrand scored the winning points in the school's big basketball game.

"Ms. Maximus said on the announcements that the Magnet Academy's basketball team has never been so good, and she said Enrique was the star!" Allie says in excitement.

"That's so cool! He must have been happy."

"He was blushing like crazy," Allie says, laughing. "I wish you could have seen it," she says wistfully.

Suddenly, I miss her and all my friends so much that a big ball of emotion starts growing in my chest. I just let Allie talk and talk. I'm afraid to say anything for a second because I'm afraid I will cry. I miss Samir and my parents and even, sort of . . . just a little, Ms. Maximus.

I have been here in Florida for nearly two weeks, and Sitti reminds me every day that I don't know how to embroider, I don't know how to cook, and I stumble over words in Arabic.

Before I came, Mama told me to be good and make Sitti happy. I have never tried so hard at something and still failed.

"Hey, we still need an idea for our Rock Stars presentation," Allie reminds me. "I'm stuck."

I tell her about the strange stones that I found in the forest here at Grand Bums. "I don't know what they are yet, but there is someone here who might help me," I tell her.

"There's an actual forest behind your grandma's building?"

"Well, not really," I say. "It's more like a pond and then a patch of trees."

"So, not a forest."

"No."

"So, why'd you call it a forest?" she asks in confusion.

"Because *forest* sounds more interesting."

She giggles. "I miss you, Farah Rocks."

. . .

Mama and Baba call me an hour before Samir's surgery.

"He will be okay, Farah," they both say, except I am tired of hearing the word *okay*. What does that even mean? Does it mean he will be back to normal, running and playing and reading? Or does it mean that he will just be alive, but different, and someone I don't even recognize?

Why don't adults just trust you enough to tell you the truth? Maybe it's because they don't know the truth.

Sitti talks to them too, and she tells them, "I will pray for him," and then hangs up the phone. She takes my hand and hauls me to the chapel, where we light candles for Samir again and she sits and prays on her rosary.

Strangely, I am calm again in the chapel with her, listening to her voice. She is repeating some prayers in Arabic. I know them from church, but I like the way they sound in her voice, like whispers hovering in the air between us.

Back in the condo, though, my worries creep back. I start to read, but then put the book down. I walk around the apartment, but there is nowhere to go, and how many times can you pace around a small room anyway? I go to my own room, close the door, and pull out the towel from under the bed. I carefully take out my mystery rocks and stare at their lines and colors.

But I have to admit, even these don't interest me right now. Not when Samir is in a hospital room, having his heart stitched back together.

Sitti knocks on my door, and I shove everything quickly under the bed.

"Why are you on the floor?" she asks.

"I, uh . . ."

"Come on," she says briskly. "It's time for a lesson."

She decides that I need to learn how to cook.

"I can make sandwiches," I say again.

"Arab girls cook. And they cook very well," she says, like it's a fact. Like it's something I have been missing. I wonder if she would stare up at Ms. Maximus, right in the eye, and tell her that cooking should be a part of the Magnet Academy classes.

She would. She would do it, I am sure.

"What should we start with?" she mutters to herself, looking around her kitchen. "Something easy."

"Hummus?" I suggest. When she nods, I open the cabinets and look around. I find eight bottles of olive oil, two bags of dry lentils, and a jar of tahine. "Where's the chickpeas?" I ask. "I don't see any cans."

"*Cans?*" She almost shouts this word, and even though she is little, she is loud. I jump back so hard that I end up sprawled on the kitchen floor.

"Yeah, *cans,*" I tell her, standing up. "Cans of chickpeas."

"Oh, my goodness, my goodness . . . ," she mutters again, and then she opens another cabinet and takes out an old coffee container. Instead of coffee, though, it's filled with hard, dry chickpeas. "We have to make them *fresh,* not from a *can,*" she mutters.

She tells me to fill a small pot with exactly four cups of chickpeas and then fill the pot with water to the brim.

"Okay, now what?" I say after I've done that.

"Now, we wait," she says.

"For what?"

"They have to soak for a couple of hours, and then we will cook them."

"Oh. Why soak them first?"

She pulls out one bean and squeezes it. "It's dry," she explains in Arabic, "so it's hard. We have to get water inside of it first, so the cooking doesn't take so long." She pauses. "Do you understand what I'm saying?"

Even though she speaks superfast, I do. I follow every word she says.

"So the water gets soaked in through the skin?" I ask her in Arabic.

She turns on the light above the stove and holds the bean under it. "Look here," she says. She pulls off her reading glasses and holds them up to the bean. Her reading glasses become like a magnifying glass, and the bean looks five times bigger. "There is a small hole, here," she points.

"I see it."

"Every bean has a hole like this. So the water gets in, and makes the bean softer. Then, when we cook it, it will cook faster."

I have to admit that is pretty cool. I start to pull other beans out of her cabinet—red beans, black beans, speckled beans. Every one of them has a hole, she says, like a little mouth to drink water.

"So what do we do while we wait?" I ask.

"We bake bread."

For the next two hours, we mix dough in two big pots. Sitti shows me how to measure carefully, how much water to add to a specific amount of flour, how much yeast and salt to mix in. "You have to measure correctly," she says.

One time, I accidentally add too much flour, and she stands there, figuring out in her head how much more yeast she now needs to add to the bowl to even it out. More math!

The dough feels so good under my hands. I have to use my shoulders and elbows when I push the big mound to get all the air pockets out. It's like playing with clay, and I think this is the first real fun I have had since I arrived.

Sitti goes to the closet and brings back a stack of clean, soft, white sheets, which we spread on the table and the counter. She shows me how to form the dough into flat ovals and lay them carefully over the sheets. I've never made pita bread before, not even with Mama.

When we have thirty pancake-like doughballs lying everywhere, Sitti covers them with more sheets, as if she is putting a baby to bed.

"Now what?"

"Now we wait." She is secretly laughing at me. I can tell by the way her lips press together, like she is trying not to crack up.

"Cooking requires a lot of waiting," I complain.

"Sometimes, you have to wait for good things."

We check on the beans, then she tells me to sweep the floor while she dusts. There is no dust anywhere, and I only collect a tiny pile of dirt in my dustpan. She bends down to look at it, and then looks at me like it's my fault there was even one speck in her house.

Finally, she says, "The dough has risen," and she fires up the oven. She explains, "The yeast here is like a hungry creature. It eats away at the bread, and it makes it less tough."

I peer at the bread. "It looks the same to me."

She clucks her tongue against her teeth, like I've said something wrong. "Inside the bread now, there are little bubbles of gas. See?" She uses her finger to show how tall the bread pancake is. "It's higher than before. The yeast created lots of air pockets inside to lift it up."

"You're talking like the yeast is alive," I say, giggling.

She glares at me. "It *is* alive."

I nod in agreement, though I think she doesn't know what she's talking about. We lay the dough pancakes on wide, metal trays and put them in the oven. As soon as one tray is done, we pull it out and slide in the next one. Sitti dumps the finished bread loaves on the white sheets so they can cool off.

There is a knock on the door, and Sitti tells me to answer it because she needs to pull out the next tray. Outside her door are Mr. Delacroix, Cal, Mitch, and Agatha.

"Fay is baking again, isn't she?"

"We can smell it in the whole building."

"You want eat?" Sitti says in her English, coming up behind me.

"Yes!"

And they all surge in, like the quacking ducks at the pond.

Sitti tells me to close the door, and I peek out into the hallway to check if anyone else is there. At the end of the hallway, his eyes closed, sniffing the aroma in the air, is Dr. Fisher.

He opens his eyes and sees me, then hurries away.

CHAPTER 10

After everyone leaves, Sitti and I try to call Mama and Baba on their cell phones, but there is no answer for a while. We clean the kitchen and start boiling the chickpeas to make hummus.

It needs to boil for one hour at least, she says, and so we sit at the counter and eat fresh bread. She puts out two bowls, one with *zeit zaytoun* and the other with *zaatar*, to dip our bread in. My friends usually think eating this looks funny, like you are eating dirt. But nothing tastes as good as dipping your bread into the *zeit* first, then into the *zaatar*. The spices stick to the oil like a magnet.

"Do you think Samir will be okay?" I ask Sitti.

"Yes," she says.

"You seem sure."

"I am."

"But nobody can be one hundred percent sure," I argue. But I don't even know why I am arguing.

"Of course not," she says. "But let's study the facts."

She closes her hand into a fist, then spreads out each finger one by one as she recites a list of facts.

One: "He has good doctors."

Two: "He has had this problem since birth, and they have been watching him."

Three: "This surgery is usually very successful."

Four: "He is a healthy boy all around."

Five: "If it doesn't work, there is another surgery that he can still do."

By the end, she has all five fingers spread out. "For these reasons, I am at least ninety-nine percent positive."

Her very scientific list makes me feel a lot better. I am grateful that she wasn't just telling me he will be "okay," without some good evidence.

Finally, my parents call us back. "Samir came through the surgery just fine!" Mama says, her voice ecstatic and giggly. "I'm sorry you called us so many times, but our phones were off. I hope you haven't spent all afternoon being worried."

I look at Sitti and realize that I *wasn't* worried the whole time because Sitti had distracted me with making hummus and baking bread.

She winks at me.

And I understand it now.

She tricked me.

Holy hummus. Nobody *ever* tricks me.

Mama and Baba say that Samir will be recovering in the hospital for a few more days, and then they will take him home, as long as he doesn't get any infections.

"Can I come home then?" I ask quickly. Before I realize what I have said, I see Sitti's face change like a cloud passing over the sun.

She understood me, even though I spoke in English. And I have hurt her feelings.

"Not yet," Mama says, her voice soft like an apology.

When I hang up, I tell Sitti, "I don't mean that I want to leave, Sitti."

"I know what you meant," she says. "You must be bored here, with just an old lady for company." She stands up and tells me to find something to do for a while, until the beans are ready to make the hummus.

Feeling bad, I take the laptop to the lobby of the main building, where Mr. Delacroix is reading on his break.

"Bored today?" he asks me.

"A little bit," I say, then I tell him that I hurt my grandmother's feelings.

"Don't worry about it," he says. "You just miss your parents and your brother. Fay knows that." That makes me feel better.

"You know, it would be good for her to come out of her condo more," he adds. "Maybe you can tell her to come with us on the lighthouse trip in a few days."

Grand Bums arranges for trips every month for the residents, he tells me. "But Fay always says she's busy,"

Mr. Delacroix says. He raises his eyebrows as if to say, "Doing *what*?"

"I'll tell her."

"I hope it works out for you to join us. I think you would really like it," he says. "The lighthouse is really special."

When I go back to her condo, Sitti is sewing quietly on the couch. I think about how much time she spends in silence. Maybe that is why she seemed upset that I wanted to leave, because with me here, there is someone else with her, someone to talk to, someone who ninety-five percent understands her when she speaks in Arabic.

I sit on the other end of the couch and go online to check that my teachers received my work last week. I check my email and see a picture of the Hope Diamond that Brian Najjarian sent me from his trip. "Farah Rocks, *this* rock is 45.52 carats! LOL! Hope Florida is fun," it reads. June Jordan also emailed me, saying that everyone in the writing club misses me.

It's weird, but it feels good to know that. My parents

are obsessed with Samir's health right now, but at least my friends haven't forgotten me.

I know Mama and Baba love me, but sometimes it's hard to be the one who doesn't need any attention or any help.

Immediately, I feel guilty for this idea. Of course they need to focus on Samir. Because the feeling is icky, I distract myself by opening Google and searching randomly for stuff. *VSD, St. Augustine Lighthouse, Haiti.* I try again to find my mystery rocks online. I go to my favorite geology website, but I cannot find them there. Then I try to Google *bark* and *rock* and *Florida*, but nothing comes up.

On a whim, I search *beans* and find that the opening in each one is called a micropyle. Sitti was right about that. On another website, I also learn that the yeast really *is* a fungus. The air pockets it makes in the bread are actually carbon dioxide.

"Making bread is actually a science," according to the site.

And Sitti was right, yeast *is* alive.

Glancing up at her, I tell her that she was correct about that, and she looks at me like I have eight heads. "Of course," she says and shrugs, then goes back to her *tatreez*.

Later, Sitti tells me to come into the kitchen. She shows me how to dump out the water that the hummus beans were in and rinse them with fresh cold water. We dump them all in her food processor, which is like a big bowl with a small set of blades  in the center. She lets me push the button, and I watch as the blades whir and make the beans creamy.

"Keep going," she says when I stop. "No lumps allowed in our hummus!"

Later, when she's satisfied, we add tahine, then salt, then cumin and lemon. Sitti lays out ten clean spoons, and we use them, one at a time, to taste the hummus.

"More lemon," I suggest. When she pours in another tablespoon and whirs it, I take a clean spoon and try again. "More salt," I say this time, and she laughs and makes the adjustment.

"Let it sit for a while," she says, watching me scoop out the hummus into a clean glass bowl.

"By the way, what's wrong with Dr. Fisher?" I ask her as I work.

She rolls her eyes. "He's a mean man."

"I don't think he's so mean," I say. I tell her about how he offered to look at the mystery rocks I found.

"He's crazy," she says, like it's an encyclopedia fact.

"Was he always like that?" I ask.

She pauses, her hand with the bread poised above the bowl of *zeit*. "No," she admits. "He was nice when his wife was alive."

Sitti tells me his wife was a school librarian who had red hair and freckles all over her face and neck and arms. A sweet woman, who died five years ago.

"What about his children?" I ask.

"He has a son who hasn't come to see him since Mrs. Fisher died," Sitti says. "I forgot all about him because I never see him."

I feel more and more sad for Dr. Fisher, thinking of his face in the hallway earlier. Grand Bums is filled with people, but it's still possible for someone to feel lonely.

We spend the rest of the evening sewing and reading and chatting quietly. And for dinner, we eat the most fabulous, creamy, zero-lumps hummus I've ever tasted.

CHAPTER 11

Sitti finds my rocks under the bed one day while she is sweeping the floor. "This towel is dirty now!" she proclaims and throws it in the trash. She won't let me polish my mystery rocks inside the condo. "Too much dirt!" she exclaims and shoos me outside.

Even though she is mad, she is kind of cute at the same time, fluttering around like a bird, flapping her wings at imaginary germs.

I follow her orders and carry my rocks outside in a plastic bag. As I walk through the main building, Cal hands me a croissant with apples baked inside. "Taste it . . . I'm experimenting."

"Holy hummus," I say. "It's scrumptious."

He gives me his huge smile and continues to the kitchen. I move on to the lobby, where Mitch sits playing dice with some other people.

"Here, Farah," he says and hands me the dice. "Throw them for me. For good luck."

I pick up the pearly dice, spotted with black holes, shake them in my palm, and toss them onto the table. They both land on the sixes. Mitch cheers while the others groan. Nearby, Agatha sits watching the game while she knits a long, colorful scarf that looks like pink and green candy ribbons.

"These are for my grandchildren," she says. "Too hot here to wear wool scarves!"

Laughing, I move on, thinking that there are so many nice people here. It's a shame Sitti doesn't hang out with them more.

Outside, I go back to the spot in the forest where I first saw the mystery rocks. And there is Dr. Fisher again, by the big palm tree, digging.

"Hello," I say cautiously, because you don't want to startle a person digging for skulls.

He looks back at me and nods, then resumes digging.

"I have those rocks," I say.

"Good." He keeps digging.

"Did you want to see them?"

"In a minute."

I watch him dig for sixty seconds before I realize he didn't mean "in an actual minute." He said it the way adults mean it, which is "whenever I am finished, and I'm not sure when that will be."

In other words, forever.

I move back to the grassy patch and look for more of my mystery rocks. There, by an exposed tree root, is something hard and rough-looking. When I swipe the dirt away with my hands, I realize it is a rock, but it's buried deep in the ground, so I walk back to Dr. Fisher.

"What?" he says gruffly.

"I need something to dig with."

He stares at me and then picks up a small shovel with a short handle. "Here."

"Thanks." In minutes, I dig up the rock and pull it out. It is wider than my palm and about as thick as a hamburger. It is rimmed with brown, but it has blue and white crusts on it. It looks like I am holding a rough painting of clouds.

"Ah, interesting," I hear Dr. Fisher say. When I look up, he is standing above me, holding a small collection of bones.

I hand him the tool. "Thanks for the shovel."

"It's a trowel," he says like he is annoyed with me. "A shovel has a long handle."

"Oh, okay! Thanks for telling me that."

He looks at me confused-funny, and then he actually grins. "You're welcome." He puts out his hand. "Let me see that."

I hand him the rock I just found, as well as the smaller ones I found a few days before.

"This is not a rock," he says, turning it in his hands. "This is petrified wood." He looks at me doubtfully. "Do you know what *petrified* means?"

"Sure, it's like when something gets turned to stone."

His eyebrows shoot up in surprise. "That's right."

"In Greek mythology, Medusa turned people to stone if they looked at her. They were petrified."

"Right. I forgot I was talking to a Minotaur." He does a weird half-laugh, like he's starting to laugh but then remembers he is supposed to be moody and stops himself just in time.

He explains that, a lot of times, wood from old tree bark or branches starts to rot, but then it gets buried in the ground. "And then water rushes in—from the swamp or from the ground—and also floods it. The water has minerals in it, and it fills the wood up," he says. "When the wood rots away, it gets replaced with the minerals. So, *this* is actually a fossil," he says.

"I thought fossils were just bones," I say.

"Oh no, plants can get fossilized too," he tells me.

"That is what you have here." He sits down on the ground and picks up the trowel. "Let's keep digging."

We find eight more rocks, big hunks of stone that look like chunks of wood, but not really. I'm excited to clean them, but I know Sitti won't let me do it in the condo.

"Fay is a clean freak, eh?"

"She covers the carpet in plastic, and even though we don't wear shoes in the condo, she even cleans the bottoms of our shoes every night, with Lysol." I shudder. "My brother gets sick a lot, so my parents disinfect everything, but Sitti Fayrouz takes it up like three hundred percent."

He half-laughs again. "My wife used to be like that." He pauses, then adds, "She would be furious to know I have a condo filled with skulls and bones right now."

He starts looking at the chunk of rock very carefully, the way people check fruit at the supermarket to see if it has bruises or spots. I can tell, even though he's hiding it, that remembering his wife makes him feel sad.

I don't know what to say, so I stay quiet. Sometimes people talk too much and it's better just to say nothing.

After a minute, he says, "I have a small wood saw in my condo. Let me take this and slice it for you, so you can see the inside. You should be able to see the lines left by the original tree."

I hand over my treasures of petrified wood to Dr. Fisher, but before he walks away, he asks, "What's wrong with your brother, by the way?"

"He has VSD."

"Ah, a hole in his heart. Did they fix it?"

I nod. "His surgery was yesterday."

He nods confidently. "He will be all right. It's a treatable condition."

And I believe him.

CHAPTER 12

Dr. Fisher does exactly what he promised he would do.

The next day, I convince Sitti to come to breakfast with me, so she can see some of the other residents at Grand Bums. They are all talking about the lighthouse trip. They keep asking her to come, but she keeps saying, "Izz too far for me."

Suddenly, Dr. Fisher comes up to me and taps my shoulder. "Come on," he says, pointing to another table. My grandmother looks at him suspiciously and asks me in Arabic what he wants.

I explain that he has some rocks to show me. She rolls her eyes and says, "Fine, but I'm watching you."

I start to take another sip of my orange juice, which Cal said he squeezed fresh this morning, but Dr. Fisher looks at me impatiently. "Come *on*," he says again, so I hurry to his table.

It looks like he has spread large gems across the tabletop. The petrified wood that he cut has been sawed into slices, like a loaf of bread, and glazed like icing on a cake. I pick one up, and I can see the growth rings in the wood. One piece glitters with blue minerals, while another piece has green and yellow tints.

"I sawed them with my special saw last night," he explains.

I take one piece and start to take it back to show it to my grandmother and Mitch. "Where are you going?" Dr. Fisher asks me.

"To show my Sitti."

"Why?"

"Because it's awesome." I pause, then ask, "Want to come with me?"

He looks uncertain, so I say, *"Come on,"* in that same bossy tone he used with me about one minute ago.

Mitch exclaims over the wood, and I pass around a few pieces. Sitti picks it up with a paper napkin, turning it over and over. She asks me what it is, and I try to explain, in my not-so-perfect Arabic, that it's a piece of wood that has become filled with minerals, and now it's more like a stone.

"Zay al hajjar?" she asks, wondering if it's like a rock now, and I nod.

Mitch starts to ask Dr. Fisher about how he cut it,

and Dr. Fisher explains about his saw. "I'd like to take a look at that," Mitch says, explaining how he used to do carpentry back in Minnesota.

Dr. Fisher says hesitantly, "You can all come back to my condo, if you like. After you've finished eating. To see my workshop."

Everyone hurries through breakfast. By the time we are heading down the hallway to the elevator, we have grown to eight people. Mr. Delacroix has joined us, as has the lady who works behind the front desk, and Mrs. Suarez, who runs the office, and Cal, who heard the chatter from the kitchen. Everyone seems excited about seeing Dr. Fisher's place.

Dr. Fisher looks nervous. I stand in the elevator next to him and whisper, "You okay?"

"These people have never been in my condo before," he mumbles. "It's weird. I've been living here for ten years."

"Well, it's about time, then. Right?" I grin when he looks surprised.

The elevator dings and we get off, heading down the third-floor hallway in a surge. He unlocks his door with his key and opens it. We enter behind him, then freeze in his foyer.

Holy hummus.

Sitti gasps and seizes my hand.

Mr. Delacroix did not exaggerate one bit.

There are shelves and shelves everywhere, lined around the living room and dining room, like a library. And on every shelf, there are either books or bones. Small animals, like squirrels and birds. There are bones that are large and unique, like one that might be a part of a rib.

And then there are skulls, in their own special section.

I walk up to a shelf, trying not to laugh while Sitti tells me if I touch the skulls, I will not be allowed to touch anything in her condo ever again. There is a small, white card in front of each skeleton or bone, labeling the animal. *Phasianidae* and *Burhunidae*, they say.

Mitch starts to read some of them aloud. Mr. Delacroix says to Dr. Fisher, "This is more than you had the last time I was here."

"I keep myself busy," Dr. Fisher says. He starts to tell everyone about the skeletons, informing them how this bird was only found in central Florida, while this bird was common across North America. Agatha asks if he would like to go bird-watching together one day, and he says, "Well, um . . . sure."

When we finish, Mr. Delacroix asks him, "Hey, you going to the lighthouse?"

"When is the trip?" Dr. Fisher asks.

"This weekend. We have a couple of spots left on the shuttle."

Dr. Fisher shrugs. "I'll think about it."

He shows Mitch his saw and how it operates. "Really neat," Mitch says. "I have some things I'm building. Maybe I can come over one day and use this?" Dr. Fisher nods.

When we all leave, everyone thanks him for showing us his collection.

"Thank you," he says, blushing again. "Thank you for coming."

CHAPTER 13

The night before the lighthouse trip, I ask Sitti if she will go, and again she says no.

"Why not?"

"Because I am busy."

"Doing what?" I want to know, and she makes the fist and opens a finger for each item.

"Cooking, cleaning, *tatreez* . . ."

"You do that every day."

"Exactly."

Holy hummus, I think. I encourage her. I tell her everyone wants her to go. Then I explain that it's good to get out and see things besides the grocery store.

Finally, I try guilt.

"Sitti, if you don't go, I can't go. I have to have an adult with me."

She grumbles. "Fine," she says. "I will go."

. . .

The next morning, she wears a new thobe, a black one with blue embroidery—there is the *bulbul* again, but also some lilies. I have been working on my own embroidery a little, and my *bulbul* is taking shape.

I have spent most mornings here exploring outside. Then, when the sun gets too hot, I come indoors to work on my homework and then on my embroidery. Sometimes, Sitti and I cook together as well, and she teaches me cool things, like calculating measurements. It reminds me of the article that explained how cooking and baking are really chemistry and science.

She still doesn't let me bring my rocks into the condo, though. I have to leave them with Dr. Fisher.

"I like your thobe," I tell her, but then I notice her

shoes. She's wearing a pair of her flip-flop sandals with leather straps. "You should wear sneakers," I suggest.

She shrugs. "I don't have sneakers," she says, and we leave the condo. It's already hot outside. As we get on the shuttle, Mr. Delacroix says that it might hit one hundred degrees. (He has to move a lot of his books out of the way because the shuttle is so full that Mitch sits up front with him.)

Sitti reaches into the front of her dress to pull out a small fan. "It's going to be too hot," she mutters in Arabic, waving the fan across her face. "I can't believe I let you talk me into this."

Then I see Dr. Fisher board the shuttle. He is wearing the same palm-leaf print shirt he wore that day on the plane, and he looks grouchier than ever.

As he walks past our seats, he looks down, sees us, and stops. He starts to scowl, but then he stops. He reaches into his pocket and pulls out a petrified wood stone, which he hands to me. "Just finished polishing this one last night," he says in his gruff voice.

"Thank you, Dr. Fisher!" I exclaim.

And then, slowly, so slowly that I wonder what's wrong with his face, he cracks a smile. He even shows his front teeth.

"We can find more, maybe, at the lighthouse. There should be some interesting rocks out there," he says.

"No more. No rocks," Sitti cuts in. I guess she understood him.

"Fay," he says to my grandmother, "I know you don't like them, but your granddaughter has a real interest—"

"Rocks so dirty!" she says stubbornly.

I sigh, and Dr. Fisher shrugs as if to say, "What can you do?" and continues to his seat.

As Mr. Delacroix drives us to the shore, where we can see the lighthouse, I think about the fact that I have been here for three weeks. I've learned to really like Sitti, and I've learned a lot from her, but there are some things that I will never understand.

The lighthouse sits on the far shore, Mr. Delacroix tells us. It was built in 1824, but it replaced an older watchtower that was built in the 1500s. I translate as much as I can for Sitti. Her nodding and the way her eyebrows scrunch together tell me that she is interested too. At one point, she reaches into her bodice and pulls out a small notebook and a pen and jots down some notes in Arabic, writing from right to left across the page.

We get off the shuttle and walk up a long, sandy road to the lighthouse, which stands like a black and white striped candle on the shore. Its red top is like a little flame. We are allowed to climb up to the top, if we want. Most of the people from Grand Bums don't want to, because they worry about the tall, steep staircase that curls around sharply.

Dr. Fisher suddenly stands next to me. "It has two hundred and nineteen steps," he says.

"Does that scare you?" I challenge him.

"Ha! Ready to go?" he asks.

"Come on!" I say, laughing.

And we climb up, up, to the very top,

until we are standing behind the glass windows. The Atlantic Ocean is spread below us like a blue picnic blanket on the ground.

"I can't believe I've missed this trip every year for the last five years," Dr. Fisher says.

"Why did you?" I ask.

He sighs and exhales deeply, like a gust of wind blowing out of his lungs. "After my wife died, I just didn't really want to go anywhere, I guess," he says. "I actually still don't. I like to explore the natural environment, add to my collection, read up on what I find." He shakes his head. "But I think now it's good to get out and have some friends too."

"I think my grandmother is starting to feel the same," I say, as I point out the window. He leans over and squints to see what I see. Sitti is standing on the sand with Mitch and Agatha and Mr. Delacroix, and they are all laughing together. Her white head scarf and her black thobe flutter with the gentle breeze that blows off the water.

We climb back down and explore for a bit with the group. I find a bunch of interesting-looking rocks under a tall tree, and I gather some up so Dr. Fisher can take pictures of them for me with his camera phone.

Sitti is standing with Dr. Fisher and Mr. Delacroix, and suddenly, she points up into a tree.

"*Bulbul!*" she says. "Izz a *bulbul!*"

"Where?" I cry, dropping the rocks in my hands, except that I drop them right on her sandaled feet.

She shrieks and takes a step backward. Her foot slips on yet another rock I have dropped. Even though Dr. Fisher and Mr. Delacroix reach for her, she topples backward, flat on her back, in the sand with a soft *plop*.

CHAPTER 14

The thing is, there really was a bulbul, I later think to myself in the shuttle. Dr. Fisher said so. "It was, from what I could tell, a red-vented *bulbul,* which is common in this part of the state," he explained.

But at that point, Sitti didn't care anymore.

Because her thobe was dirty.

And her toes hurt.

And her back was sore.

And she was as mad at me as a pot of boiling chickpeas.

"Why do you carry big rocks? Why do you need them?" she asked me over and over on the ride home.

I told her the same answer, "Because I collect rocks, and I'm curious." But that never seemed to satisfy her.

When we return from the lighthouse, Sitti hobbles out of the shuttle in pain. Mr. Delacroix and Dr. Fisher help her off the shuttle and into the condo.

I'm really upset when I see the pain in her face. *She's so little,* I think when I compare her to the two men, who tower over her like two big lighthouses. They walk across the plastic runners on the carpeted floor and help her into her room. A few minutes later, she hobbles out, wearing a clean thobe.

The men help her sit on the couch while I bring a chair from the kitchen so she can prop up her foot.

"No!" she says to me sharply in Arabic. "I can't put my feet on the cushion."

So I bring a plastic trash bag and drape that over the seat, and then she's willing to put up her foot. I pull off her sandal, and her ankle is puffy and swollen. The nail on her big toe is cracked from the rock that I dropped on it.

The two men leave while I get her a glass of water with lemon and mint. She shouts instructions at me from the couch into the kitchen. "Put in just three mint leaves! Squeeze the lemon!" I do as she says, and soon I have a tall glass of water sitting before her.

She tells me that the thobe will have to be cleaned very carefully, washed by hand, in fact. From the look on her face, I know she means that I will be the one to do it.

And I will do it, because I feel bad that she got hurt.

There is a knock on the door, and Dr. Fisher is back. Sitti motions toward his shoes. He slips them off and leaves them by the door, then comes in to sit down on one of the chairs. When I ask if he'd like some water, he says he would, and then he passes Sitti a book.

When I return with his glass, I see her paging through it. It's a book of birds, and specifically, a book on Passerine Songbirds. That's what it says on the cover, just so you know. She has the book open to a page where I can see a *bulbul,* with a red spot of feathers near its tail.

"That's the red-vented *bulbul* she saw today," Dr. Fisher says. "I remembered I had a book on them."

"These izz from my country," she tells him, "but izz yellow."

"Yes, the yellow-vented one is not found here in North America," he begins to explain. I move to pass him the water, but I trip over the leg of the chair that Sitti is resting her foot on. I lurch forward.

He shrieks. I shriek. Sitti shrieks.

But in the end, there is no help for it.

Dr. Fisher has a glass of water splashed all over his lap, and when he stands and turns to look at the chair cushion, I can see the damp stain all over the back of his shorts.

Holy hummus.

Again.

But this time, instead of glaring at me, he snorts.

Like a Minotaur.

By the third snort, I realize that he's laughing.

"I'll go change my clothes," he says, "and I'll be back."

Sitti mutters that at least I didn't spill the water on her couch.

. . .

Later, I put a new bag of ice on Sitti's ankle while she fiddles with her cell phone. She keeps trying to call my mom, but every time she pushes the number eight, her finger hits the five instead and she hangs up, then starts again.

Finally she gets through to my mom, who tells us that Samir is doing great. He will be coming home in three more days, and I can fly back home myself next week.

"Your ticket is flexible," Mama explains. "You can use it whenever you want."

"Can I stay just a few more days?" I ask her. "I'm having a lot of fun with Sitti."

Sitti's eyes mist over, and she leans over, mumbling at me to adjust the ice bag, but I know she is happy.

CHAPTER 15

Being back in Harbortown is a wonderful feeling.

Being back in my own room is amazing.

Being at the dinner table with my brother Samir, and seeing him eat like a horse, is not something I can describe.

Just kidding. Of course I can.

When I see Samir eating like a Minotaur, I feel relieved and happy and sappy and weepy all at once. Because I know he is healthy and getting better all the time. The doctors said the hole in his heart is fixed. He might even be able to sign up for soccer this summer.

Allie comes over for dinner too, and I tell everyone about my time in Florida with Sitti. I tell them about Dr. Fisher, and the spilled soda, and Mr. Delacroix, and Cal the cook, and the trip to the St. Augustine Lighthouse.

I also pass out some souvenirs.

For Mama, I have a bag of dried hummus beans. "Because I plan to help you cook more now that I know some of Sitti's recipes. We can start with hummus."

For Baba, I have a piece of fabric, embroidered with my *bulbul*. He recognizes it. "This is the same bird that all the ladies wore on their dresses back home, that all the billows and tabestries were decorated with." I tell him that I'm going to embroider some pillows for our house, to remind him of where he grew up.

For Samir, I give him a tiny, polished bird skeleton that Dr. Fisher let me have. He helped me wrap it up in bubble paper so it wouldn't break on the flight home. "Can I keep it in my room?" he asks Mama and Baba, who nod and say sure without hesitation.

For Allie, I have a chunk of petrified wood. She and Baba exclaim over it, and they ask me all the questions I asked Dr. Fisher. Baba gets the family iPad and searches for it on Google. We find a lot more pictures and information. I've brought home six pieces with me, which Dr. Fisher also helped me wrap carefully.

"You know what I'm thinking, right?" Allie says, holding one piece of wood up to the light to watch the minerals glitter.

"What?"

When she tells me, I exclaim, "Holy hummus! What a great idea!"

. . .

The Magnet Academy Rock Stars festival takes place only two weeks after I get back from Florida, but Allie and I are ready.

We spread a blue cloth on the table and set up our trifold, which is decorated in big blue letters with our title: *WOOD YOU BE PETRIFIED?*

We have pasted charts about petrified wood, the minerals, even a timeline of how the process happens. I emailed Dr. Fisher in Florida for some of the information, and he sent me back links to cool websites that helped us with our research.

He also told me that Sitti signed up for a trip to go with the residents of Grand Bums to Cape Canaveral to visit the Kennedy Space Center. She even asked Mr. Delacroix to drive her to the store so that she could buy a pair of sneakers.

"I think your visit did her a world of good," he says in his email. "I think it did a world of good for me too." He tells me that his son is planning to come and visit him in the summer for two weeks. He doesn't add more than that, but I can imagine how happy that makes him.

Ms. Maximus walks around with the judges, who are the science teachers, to examine every exhibit. They stop at our table and spend a lot of time looking at our charts and examining the pieces of polished petrified wood we have laid out as samples. "These are great samples of petrified wood," says Mr. Beaker, who is one of the coolest teachers in the school.

"Fascinating," says another teacher. "Where did you discover these?"

"She spent a month in Florida," says Ms. Maximus, looking at me strangely. I think, maybe, she is smiling. Ms. Maximus always looks so grim and fierce that this smile is more like a little crack in her mouth. "She managed to keep up with all of her schoolwork and do a little exploring of her new environment, as you can see."

"What is your name?" asks the teacher. "I teach eighth grade, so I haven't had you as a student yet."

"This is Farah Hajjar," says Ms. Maximus. "We call her Farah Rocks, because . . . she really does."

Tatreez Artwork

Palestinians call the art of embroidery *tatreez*. Every Palestinian village has its own symbols and designs. It works like a code! The symbols on a dress or tapestry can tell you which village or town the artist is from.

One of the most famous and oldest *tatreez* designs used is the Star of Bethlehem. It has eight points and represents the ancient Palestinian town of Bethlehem.

Tatreez uses traditional cross-stitch, which takes time to learn. However, you can make your own Star of Bethlehem *tatreez* artwork!

Supplies:

- 1 sheet of 8.5-x-11-inch graph paper
- pencil
- red marker
- markers of three other colors
- glue

- scissors
- ruler
- 1 sheet of 8.5-x-11-inch cardboard or sturdy paper
- 1 sheet of red construction paper

Steps

1. On your graph paper, make a replica of the eight-pointed Star of Bethlehem following the guide on page 136. Put a small dot on each square. (Note that each row of the star's eight points is built with five "stitches.")

2. Using your red marker, put an x in each box that contains the points of the star.

3. Using your other colors, "x" in the rest of the graph paper until you have a design around the star.

4. Glue the graph paper onto the cardboard

5. Use your construction paper to cut two 1-x-11-inch strips and two 1-x-8.5-inch strips. Glue them around the borders of the graph paper to form a frame around the edge. Now your star is sitting in a lovely frame. Decorate it with your markers!

❀ Glossary of Arabic Words ❀

asfour—bird

habibti—my love (to a girl)

inshallah—God willing

magloubeh—meaning "upside down," a dish of rice and meat that is cooked in a pot and flipped into a serving tray

qahwah—coffee

sah—correct

tatreez—embroidery, an essential part of Palestinian culture

thobe—a traditional, usually embroidered gown worn by Palestinian women

waraq—paper or card

yallah—come on

zaatar—ground-up blend of thyme, salt, and sesame seeds

zaytoun—olive

zeit—oil

Glossary

asthma (AZ-muh)—a condition that causes a person to wheeze and have difficulty breathing

bodice (BOD-uhs)—the upper part of a piece of clothing between the waist and the shoulders

fungus (FUHN-guhs)—a single-celled organism that lives by breaking down and absorbing the natural material it lives in

geology (jee-AHL-uh-jee)—the study of minerals, rocks, and soil

grimace (GRIM-uhs)—a twisting of the face or features in disapproval or pain

howlite (HOW-lite)—a borate mineral, white in color, discovered by and named after scientist Henry How in 1868

labyrinth (LAB-uh-rinth)—a maze of winding passages that may be difficult to find the way out of

micropyle (MYE-kruh-pile)—a tiny opening in a seed that is used for water absorption during germination

mineral (MIN-ur-uhl)—a substance found in nature that is not made by a plant or animal

minor (MYE-ner)—a person under the age of eighteen

Minotaur (MIN-uh-tar)—a monster in Greek mythology that is shaped half like a man and half like a bull

mythology (mih-THAHL-uh-jee)—old or ancient stories told again and again that help connect people with their past

ornithologist (or-nuh-THAHL-uh-jist)—a scientist who studies birds

Passeriformes (pas-ser-ih-FOR-meez)—the largest order of birds, including many backyard birds such as crows, cardinals, and sparrows

Phasianidae (fay-see-AN-ih-dee)—the bird family that includes turkeys, grouse, pheasants, and partridges

petrified (PEH-truh-fyed)—turned into stone

rosary (ROH-zuh-ree)—a special string of beads used for prayer in certain religions

ABOUT THE AUTHOR

Susan Muaddi Darraj is an award-winning author of more than ten books, including two short story collections. She is an associate professor of English at Harford Community College in Bel Air, Maryland, and she also teaches creative writing at Johns Hopkins University and Fairfield University. A native Philadelphian, Susan currently lives in Baltimore. She loves books, coffee, and baseball, and she's mildly obsessed with stationery supplies.

ABOUT THE ILLUSTRATOR

Illustrator and graphic designer Ruaida Mannaa completed her undergraduate studies at the Universidad del Norte in her hometown in Colombia. She went on to pursue a Master's degree in illustration at the Savannah College of Art and Design. She grew up in a multicultural family, surrounded by different languages, loud parties, and delicious food, and she finds great inspiration for her art in culture and cultural exchange.

Farah Rocks